SOMETHING BEAUTIFUL

For my daughter Georgia,
for the kids at P.S. 291 in the Bronx,
and in memory of a caring child,
Kia Carnegie
— S.D.W.

To Nanna
— C.S.

SOMETHING BEAUTIFUL

Sharon Dennis Wyeth

Illustrated by
Chris K. Soentpiet

When I look through my window, I see a brick wall. There is trash in the courtyard and a broken bottle that looks like fallen stars.

There is writing in the halls of my building.
On the front door, someone put the word *Die*.

Where I walk I pass a lady whose home is a big cardboard carton. She sleeps on the sidewalk, wrapped in plastic.

I run past a dark alley, where Mommy told me I must never stop.

Behind a fence, there is a garden without any flowers.

Mommy said that everyone should have something beautiful in their life.

Where is my something beautiful?

BEAUTIF

The teacher taught me the word in school.
I wrote it in my book. *B-E-A-U-T-I-F-U-L.*
Beautiful! I think it means: something that
when you have it, your heart is happy.

I go to Miss Delphine's Diner. "Hi there, sugar pie," says Miss Delphine. "What are you up to?"

"I'm looking for a something beautiful," I tell her.

"Sit down for a minute," she says as she goes to the grill. She puts on fish. The fish sizzles. Miss Delphine makes it into a sandwich.

"There's nothing more beautiful tasting than my fried fish sandwiches," she tells me. My teeth sink in.

"Mm! This is good!"

When I go back outside, I see some of my friends. "Do you have a something beautiful?" I ask them.

"I have my jump rope," says Sybil.

"I have my beads," says Rebecca.

"Check out my new shoes," says Jamal.

"My fruit store is one beautiful store," says Mr. Lee.

"You do have nice apples," I say.

"Thank you," says Mr. Lee. "Take one!"

"Watch my moves," says Marc, playing ball in the playground.
"Hear my sounds!" says Georgina, dancing on the sidewalk.

"Touch this smooth stone," says old Mr. Sims, sitting on his front steps. "All these years, I have carried it in my pocket."

Through the big window in the launderette, I see
Aunt Carolyn, holding baby Carl.
"And where are you off to, little miss?" she asks me.
"I am looking for something beautiful," I say.
She hands me Carl and folds up the clothes. I tickle
Carl and he giggles. He makes me giggle too.
"My baby's laugh is something beautiful," says
Aunt Carolyn.

I go back home and sit down on my stoop.
I look at the trash in my courtyard. I see the
word *Die* on my door.

I go upstairs and get a broom and a sponge
and some water.

I pick up the trash. I sweep up the glass. I
scrub the door very hard. When *Die* disappears,
I feel powerful.

Someday I'll plant flowers in my courtyard.

I'll invite all my friends to see.

I will give a real home and a real bed to the lady who sleeps in a cardboard carton. She will sing and I will hear her song.

Mommy comes home from work. She gives me a great big hug.

"Do you have something beautiful?" I ask her.

"Of course," she says. "I have you."

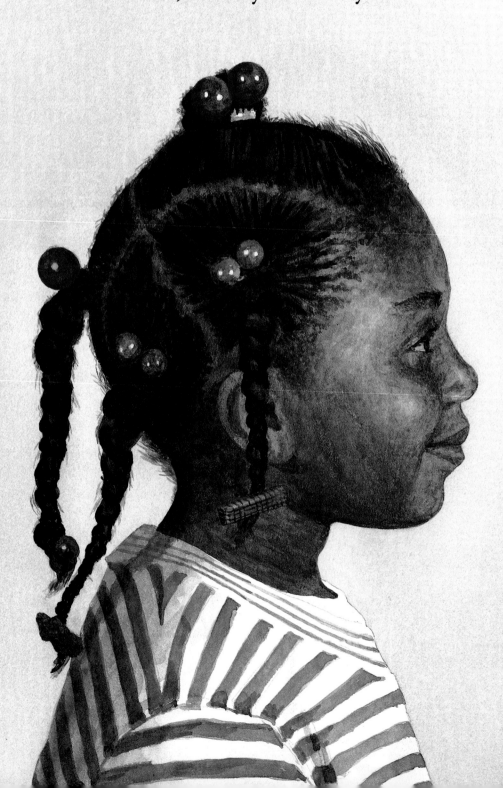

AUTHOR'S NOTE

When I was eight years old, I asked my mother, whose name was Evon, for "something beautiful." She gave me one of her wedding gifts: a small white china pitcher with a golden handle and a golden rose embossed on it. I put the pitcher on my windowsill so I wouldn't have to look at the alley outside. I called the pitcher my something beautiful. When Mommy gave me the gift, she cautioned me not to forget that I already had something even more beautiful—the something beautiful I had inside. I still have the little pitcher. I keep it next to my bed. It helps keep alive the memory of childhood and my mother's love.

Published by Bantam Doubleday Dell Publishing Group, Inc., 1540 Broadway, New York, New York 10036

Doubleday and the portrayal of an anchor with a dolphin are trademarks of Bantam Doubleday Dell Publishing Group, Inc.

Text copyright © 1998 by Sharon Dennis Wyeth
Illustrations copyright © 1998 by Chris K. Soentpiet

Library of Congress Cataloging-in-Publication Data
Wyeth, Sharon Dennis.
    Something beautiful / Sharon Dennis Wyeth ; illustrated by Chris
K. Soentpiet.
        p.   cm.
    Summary: When she goes looking for "something beautiful" in her
city neighborhood, a young girl finds beauty in many different forms.
    ISBN 0-385-32239-9
    [1. City and town life—Fiction. 2. Afro-Americans—Fiction.]
I. Soentpiet, Chris K., ill. II. Title
PZ7.W9746So 1998
[E]—dc21   96-37872
                                        CIP
                                      AC

The text of this book is set in 18-point Adobe Garamond.
Book design by Ericka Meltzer
Manufactured in the United States of America
October 1998
10 9 8 7 6 5 4 3 2